CERTIFICATE CANCELED
Date
Journal Folio
Certificate Number
Number of Shares
Fraction
Date
Journal Folio

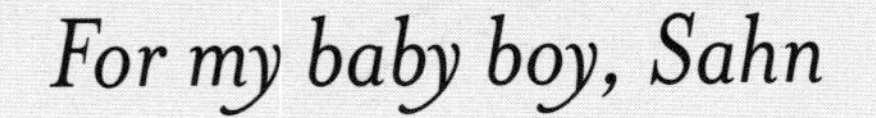

For my baby boy, Sahn

Distributed in Canada by D&M Publishers, Inc.
Color separations by Embassy Graphics Ltd.
Printed in May 2010 in China by South China Printing Co. Ltd.,
Dongguan City, Guangdong Province
Designed by Jay Colvin
First edition, 2010
1 3 5 7 9 10 8 6 4 2

www.fsgkidsbooks.com

Library of Congress Cataloging-in-Publication Data
Yum, Hyewon.
There are no scary wolves / Hyewon Yum.— 1st ed.
p. cm.
Summary: A little boy is afraid of scary wolves without his mother, but when she is holding his hand he is much braver.
ISBN: 978-0-374-38060-1
[1. Fear—Fiction. 2. Mothers and sons—Fiction. 3. Imagination—Fiction. 4. Wolves—Fiction.] I. Title.

PZ7.Y89656Th 2010
[E]—dc22

2009014144

there are no scary wolves

Hyewon Yum

Frances Foster Books
Farrar Straus Giroux / New York

I love to go outside.

But Mom never wants to go out when I do. She's always too busy.

"We'll go out later," she says, "when I've finished my work."

"Why can't I go out now?"

"Because you can't go out alone. It's too dangerous for a little boy like you."

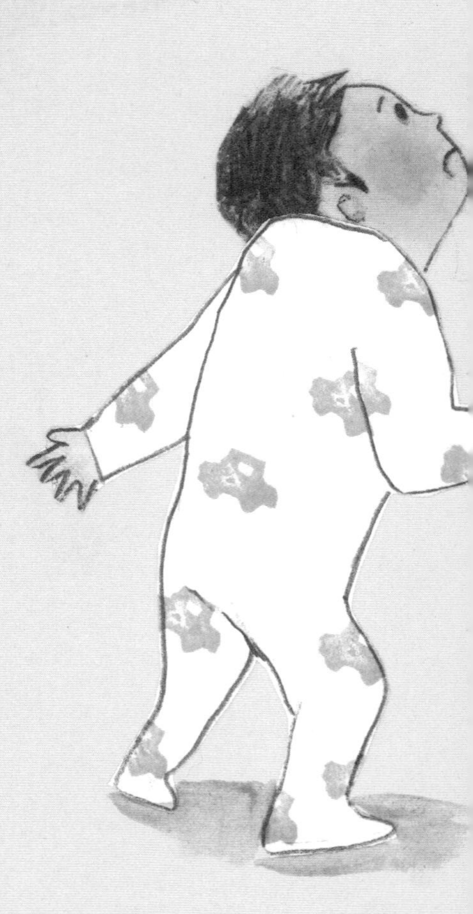

“No, I’m a big boy! I’m not even afraid of scary wolves.”

DAILY NE
AMES gains
approval of

Today Mom says, "Why don't you go get dressed? We're going out. We'll go to the Chinese restaurant to get your favorite noodles. And since you've been such a good boy this morning, we will stop by the toy store on our way home."

I put on my sweater and boots and cape.
This is the best day, and I feel absolutely big.

I'm all ready to go, but Mom can't find her keys.

"Wait right here," she says. "I'll be just a minute."

I wait one minute.

Two minutes.

Five minutes.

Mom is still looking for her keys, and I'm getting tired of waiting! I'm getting hungry for my favorite noodles.

I'm sure I could find the Chinese restaurant by myself. I'm a big boy!

HERE
CHINESE RESTAURANT
TURN RIGHT
MY HOUSE
TURN
LEFT

Oh, no! There's a scary wolf in the Chinese restaurant.
I'm not even hungry anymore.

I make a fast escape.

TOYS
TOYS
OPEN
LOST CAT
SUNDAY PARTY
DE LUXE

Oh, no! A scary wolf is in the toy store, too!

Bakery

Scary wolves are everywhere!

Mom is still looking for her keys.

Finally she finds them.
“Let’s go,” she says.
But now I don’t want to go.

"I'm too little to go out," I say. "I'm afraid of the scary wolves."

Mom looks me in the eye and says, "You're a big boy, and I'll be right there with you."

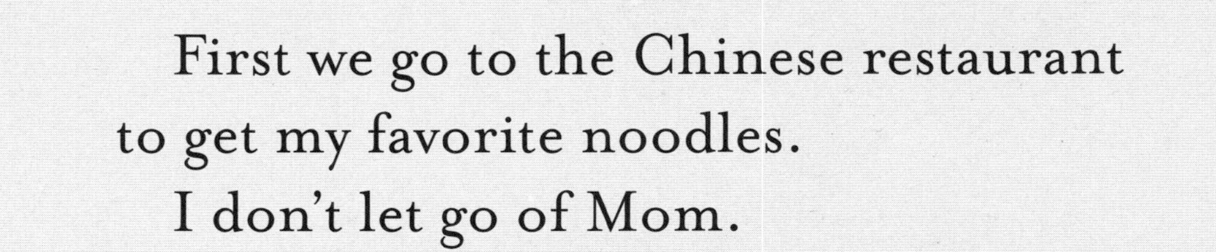

First we go to the Chinese restaurant to get my favorite noodles.

I don't let go of Mom.

But the wolf is gone!

Next we go to the toy store.
The scary wolf isn't there, either!
Mom buys me a red racing car.

PUSH
WELCOME

And then we go home.
And there are no scary wolves anywhere!

OLFVILLE
REWARD
SALE

TOTAL,
6 7 8
TOTAL
BY WHOM SURRENDERED
CERTIFICATE CANCELED
Ledger Folio
No. Certificate